Sandra Markle

SCIENCE

TO
THE
RESCUE

ATHENEUM · 1994 · New York
MAXWELL MACMILLAN CANADA Toronto
MAXWELL MACMILLAN INTERNATIONAL New York · Oxford · Singapore · Sydney

To my husband Bill with love because he always comes to my rescue

The author would especially like to thank the following for sharing their expertise and enthusiasm:

Jack Beven, Meteorologist, Hurricane Center, Coral Gables, Florida

Dave Bennet, Technology Manager for Robotics, Battelle's Pacific Northwest Laboratories

Ronald P. Verkon, Senior Applications Engineer, Corning, Inc.

Atheneum
Macmillan Publishing Company
866 Third Avenue
New York, NY 10022

Maxwell Macmillan Canada, Inc.
1200 Eglinton Avenue East
Suite 200
Don Mills, Ontario M3C 3N1

Macmillan Publishing Company is part of the Maxwell Communication Group of Companies.

First edition
Printed in Hong Kong on recycled paper

10 9 8 7 6 5 4 3 2 1
The text of this book is set in Meridian.

Library of Congress Cataloging-in-Publication Data

Markle, Sandra.
  Science to the rescue / by Sandra Markle.—1st ed.
      p.   cm.
  Includes index.
  Summary: Presents ways science is being used today to meet problems such as the necessity for precision surgery, atmospheric pollution, and overpopulation of coastal cities. Provides hands-on projects for the reader and stresses the importance of the scientific method.
  ISBN 0-689-31783-2
      1. Science projects—Juvenile literature.   2. Science—Juvenile literature.
  [1. Science.   2. Science projects.]   I. Title.
  Q164.M2753 1994   92-41096
  507.8—dc20

CONTENTS

INTRODUCTION

Science is an adventure. There's often a lot of hard work involved, but it's detective work, with all the exciting drama of tracking down leads and playing hunches. There may be frustration when a lead proves to be a dead end or an idea doesn't work as hoped. But when a problem is finally—successfully—solved, the feeling is wonderful!

In this book you'll discover a number of the creative ways in which science is solving real-life problems and making an important difference. There are plenty of challenges for you too. There are hands-on activities to investigate, problem-solving situations to tackle, and opportunities to invent.

Luckily, scientists don't have to start from scratch every time they tackle a new problem, and you won't either. You'll be able to use your past experiences, dig up facts that have already been discovered, and use technology that has already been developed. Then you can move forward, modifying, improving, and possibly even making new discoveries.

Here's a five-step approach that will help you follow through from beginning to end as you tackle any problem-solving situation.

1. Start by finding out everything you can about the problem. To do that, you'll want to observe carefully and write down a detailed description of your observations. You'll probably also want to talk to people to check out what they've observed and read anything that's been written on the subject. The very latest information is most likely to be found in magazines and newspapers.

2. Brainstorm. Spend some time looking over the information you've collected and think about possible solutions to the problem. Set a time limit for brainstorming, though, to keep yourself moving along on the project.

3. Use your own past experiences and the experiences of others. You probably learned a good deal about what others have done when you researched the problem. Use these and your own experiences to evaluate your list of possible solutions. Which one do you think is the most likely to produce the best results? Think about the technology that's currently available for you to use to be sure you'll have the tools to accomplish your plan. Be sure the materials and equipment you want to use are things you have on hand, can borrow easily, or can purchase inexpensively.

4. Experiment to test the solution you chose.

5. Finally, analyze the results of your test. Did it solve the problem? If not, what else could you try? Did things work as well as you hoped? If not, what improvements could you make? Keep trying until you feel you've found the best possible solution for the problem. Or if you decide you've gone as far as you can with the technology and materials available to you, draw plans for what else you think should be done.

Remember, you don't have to work alone. Scientists often tackle problems in teams. It can help to share ideas, and it can make tracking down leads even more fun. Scientists sometimes compete with one another to see who can be the first to solve a problem. You and your friends might enjoy doing that too.

This book is packed with science discoveries that will amaze you and with challenges designed to keep you thinking, investigating, and inventing. Here's your chance to share the excitement of being a scientist!

USING GOOD SCIENTIFIC METHOD

In an experiment, there are always three kinds of variables or things that could change. The **manipulated variable** is the one thing being changed on purpose to see what effect this change will have. The **responding variable** is whatever change occurs as a result of the experiment; it's what's measured and analyzed. The **controlled variables** are everything else that could just happen to change during an experiment and affect the outcome.

Here are some tips on how to experiment that you'll want to follow to be sure the results you observe are what's likely to happen every time and not just a freak occurrence.

• Plan carefully so you change or manipulate just one variable as you experiment. To do this you'll need to think about everything that could affect the results. It could be the size of your test containers or the materials you use. It could even be the temperature of the room in which you perform the test or the way you measure the results. A lot of things can have an effect, but these conditions all need to be exactly the same so you can be sure that only the one change you've made is really what caused the results you measure.

• Make certain the variable you manipulate is changed in a precise, orderly way. For example, if you're testing whether adding fertilizer affects how tall a plant grows, give some plants a little fertilizer, others a little more, and others a lot. In this case, you might add one-fourth teaspoon of fertilizer to a cup of water for the first set of plants, one-half teaspoon of fertilizer to a cup of water for the second, and so forth.

• Always have at least three in each test group. Or repeat each test at least three times. The test results you get one time could be just a freak occurrence.

• Always have a control. The control undergoes all parts of the experiment except that no variable is changed. If you were checking the effect of fertilizer on growth, for example, the control plants wouldn't be given any fertilizer.

• Decide before you test exactly what results you're going to measure. Then make all measurements as exact as possible.

More than twenty thousand people live on Port Island in Kobe, Japan. You can see the tall office buildings. There are also sports facilities, homes, parks, and factories. Before 1966, though, there wasn't anything here. In fact, there wasn't even an island. So what happened to create Port Island?

PROBLEM The populations of coastal cities are growing. The cities need to expand, but they've run out of land.

SCIENCE RESCUE Build artificial offshore islands.

That's what they're doing in the Netherlands, India, Israel, Singapore, and especially in Japan. The islands may be small or, like Port Island in Osaka Bay off Kobe, Japan, they can be huge. Port Island is over two thousand acres, and if more land is needed, it could grow even larger.

How do people go about constructing an artificial offshore island (AOI)? There are several different design techniques. The key factors are: 1) where the island will be located and 2) for what purpose it will be used. Port Island was built through a process called reclamation, which mimics the way real islands develop. First, a strong wall was constructed, extending from the seafloor to the surface. Then dirt was dug out of a nearby hilly area and transported by an overhead conveyor belt to the bay. There it was loaded on barges and hauled to the building site. As the dirt was dumped inside the containment wall, the water it displaced was released through special drainage channels. As you might imagine, millions of tons of earth were needed to complete Port Island, which is about thirty-nine feet above sea level at its highest point.

Building and living on this type of island isn't really any different than living on a natural island. The island won't rock with the waves, but it will shake if there's an earthquake.

Artificial offshore islands not only provide a way to expand a coastal city—they improve the city's onshore areas too. Noisy and often ugly to look at, ports for loading and unloading ships can be moved offshore, freeing the city's waterfront land for residential communities and parks. AOIs can also help protect coastal regions. For example, Coal Island in Japan's Inland Sea is used to stockpile coal for twenty different coal-burning power plants in nearby cities. This saves land near the power plants for other uses and eliminates coal-dust pollution on shore.

While artificial offshore islands provide more living space for people and improve coastal cities, special efforts have to be taken to ensure they don't harm marine animals living in these same areas. The Japanese, for example, built underwater dams to control destructive currents that otherwise might have caused erosion. With currents reduced, suspended nutrients also settled to the bottom, forming rich feeding areas for fish. Another island was built on a specially supported platform to hold it above a seabed breeding ground.

When oil wells need to be drilled out in the ocean, man-made rigs become working islands. This one off the coast of Louisiana is a special type called a jackup rig. Jackup rigs are used in waters up to three hundred feet deep. They're either self-propelled or towed to a site. Then steel legs are lowered to anchor the rigs to the seafloor. Jackup rigs work like an elevator, so they can lift the platform on its legs during storms to keep it safely above water.

The tall tower you can see is the drilling rig. What looks like a giant Frisbee is a helicopter landing pad. There are also living quarters for the crew. Imagine what it would be like to live and work on one of these man-made drilling islands—especially during a storm. (COURTESY OF AMERICAN PETROLEUM INSTITUTE)

Like reclaimed islands, those sitting on supporting posts aren't affected by waves but are threatened by earthquakes. They're also permanent. Some AOIs are designed strictly as work sites. Such an island may be attached to legs set into the ocean floor or it may simply be anchored like a ship. Floating islands are the least likely to be damaged by earthquakes. They can also be located in very deep water, where it would be too expensive and too difficult to anchor legs. And a floating island can be easily towed from site to site as needed. The main drawback to a floating island is that, like a ship, the island will pitch and roll with the waves.

TACKLE THE CHALLENGE

YOUR CHALLENGE: *Draw a diagram and build a model artificial island that is both earthquake-resistant and not affected by wave motion.*

Before you begin, here are two model artificial islands you can build to understand the two basic types of AOIs. Work outdoors where it won't matter if you're messy. Use a cake pan for a really miniature sea.

1. Mimicking Nature: This island, like those off the coast of Japan, will be built from the seafloor up. You'll need scissors, an empty one- or two-liter plastic soft-drink bottle, and about eight cups of soil or sand. Fill the cake pan about half full of water. Cut the ends off the soft-drink bottle to create a cylinder. Trim it so the cylinder will extend just above the surface of the water when you set one end on the bottom of the cake pan. Have a friend hold this cylinder upright in the water with one end on the bottom. Pour soil or sand into the cylinder, displacing the water to create the artificial island.

2. Floating Island: This type of island, which is most often used in very deep water (as deep as six thousand feet), is really a giant anchored raft. You'll need a clean Styrofoam meat tray, sixteen inches of monofilament fishing line, a sharp pencil, and four metal washers. Fill the cake pan nearly full of water. Trim the Styrofoam tray if necessary so it will fit to float on the mini-ocean. Cut the fishing line into four equal lengths. Tie one washer to each line. Use the pencil to poke four holes in the tray, one to a side, about an inch from the edge. Thread the free end of one line through each hole, looping it over the edge and tying a knot. Set the "island" afloat, letting down the washers to anchor it.

SEE FOR YOURSELF

To see what happens to these basic island designs during earthquakes, shake the cake pan. To see what happens when the waves are high, wiggle your hand in the water to create waves. Now work on your design for a new and improved AOI—one that is both wave- and earthquake resistant. You may want to devise a way to modify one of the model islands you built or develop a completely new island design.

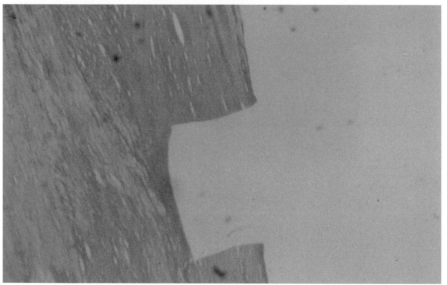

(COURTESY OF IBM RESEARCH)

Lasers have become important tools for a surgeon. An incision made by a laser is much more exact and less damaging to the surrounding tissue than one made by a surgical knife or scalpel. The top photo shows a blood vessel which has been cut with a standard surgical laser.

Now, take a close look at the second picture. It shows a blood vessel that was cut with a special kind of laser called an excimer laser. Can you see why this kind of laser makes an even better surgical tool?

PROBLEM Some surgery requires great precision, and damage to surrounding tissues could have a serious effect.

SCIENCE RESCUE Use an excimer laser.

To understand why an excimer laser is an improvement over a standard laser and how light can be used to perform surgery in the first place, you first need to know what laser light is. And to do that you need to learn some basics about light.

First, light is a form of energy. Particles of light energy called photons, like water, travel in waves. The wavelength of light is the distance from one crest to the next or from one trough to the next. The frequency of light is the number of crests or troughs per second. Visible light is the wavelengths and frequencies that the human eye can detect.

Light waves normally travel in straight lines. If the light strikes something, though, it is reflected, passes through, or is absorbed. When light passes through something, the wave becomes refracted, or bent, because it changes speed. Light is slowed slightly by air, even more by water, and quite a bit by glass. If you've ever seen white light, as visible light is called, passed through a prism, you've also discovered something else. White light is actually made up of a whole spectrum of different-colored lights. Each of these colors of light has its own wavelength and frequency, so each is slowed at a slightly different rate when it passes through the prism. This makes the colored lights separate into a visible spectrum—red, orange, yellow, green, blue, indigo, and violet. Red has the lowest frequency and violet has the highest frequency.

In 1960 American scientist Theodore Mai-

man developed a way to generate a light beam that was a single wavelength and frequency. That meant the light wave was a very narrow beam because all the wave crests and troughs were synchronized. The beam also remained narrow over a distance instead of spreading out the way light waves usually do, so the beam of light energy could be aimed at a target to cut or drill or slice.

Laser light, like this beam, is always only one wavelength and frequency and so only one color. The particular color depends on the material used to generate the laser light. In this case, the green laser light was generated by a crystal of a special material called neodymium yttrium aluminum garnet.

(COURTESY OF GENERAL ELECTRIC)

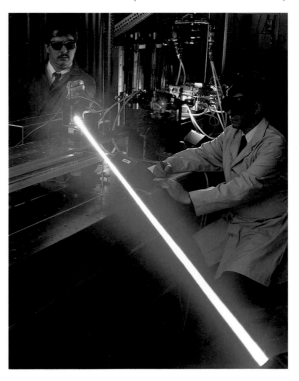

Single wavelength and frequency light beams were named laser light. Laser stands for *l*ight *a*mplification by *s*timulated *e*mission of *r*adiation, a name that describes how laser light is generated. The process begins when an intense flash of light is shot through a certain material, such as a ruby crystal or a colored dye, inside an enclosed space. Some of the atoms, or building blocks, of this material are stimulated by this light energy to give off a burst of energy of their own—a photon. Since these photons can't escape, they strike other atoms, causing them to give off photons too. The ends of the container are mirrored to reflect the photons back into the material, causing them to bump into still other atoms, helping the chain reaction to continue. Since all the photons that are produced are exactly the same amount of energy, the light waves that form all have the same wavelength and frequency.

The energy level within the container might build up until it explodes except for one thing: One of the mirrored ends isn't completely sealed, so when the energy level is great enough, the light energy bursts through this end in the form of a laser beam.

You already discovered that since laser light can be aimed and its energy level controlled it can be used very precisely as a surgical tool. Now, how is an excimer laser different from a typical laser—and better?

An excimer laser, like other lasers, is a single-frequency light beam and can be focused with extreme precision. An excimer laser, though, is ultraviolet light, light that has an even higher frequency, or number of waves per second, than any of the light we can see. Ultraviolet light has just the right frequency to break apart the chemical bonds that hold together molecules—the groups of

atoms that make up any substance. As soon as enough molecular bonds are broken, the molecules break loose and fly away from the remaining material at great speeds—too fast to produce heat that could cause damage. This process of "blasting" away molecules is so precise, in fact, that an excimer laser can remove tissue layers as thin as 1/25,000th of an inch.

An excimer laser is so precise that it was possible to carve notches in this human hair.

(COURTESY OF IBM RESEARCH)

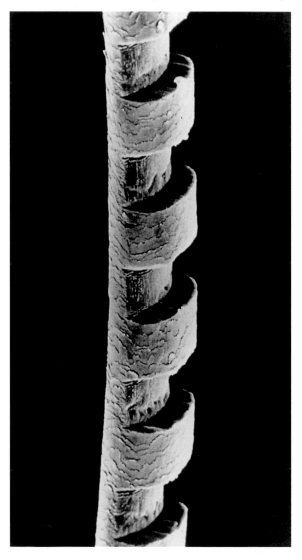

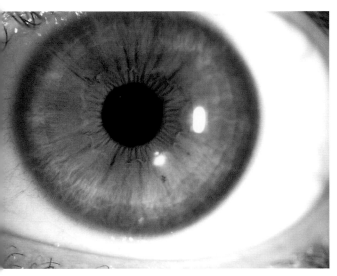

Light rays entering the eye are mechanically brought into focus as they pass through the cornea, the glassy window-like covering of the eye, and the lens. When the light strikes light-sensitive cells on the retina, the thin membrane lining the inside of the eyeball, signals are transmitted to the brain where they are interpreted. Then the brain sends out signals of its own that are understood as ''seeing.'' Of course, all this happens very quickly. In fact, it happens almost instantly.

(COURTESY OF DR. KEITH THOMPSON, EMORY EYE CENTER)

To see clearly, the eye's cornea and lens must bend light rays so they converge precisely on the retina's light-sensitive cells. The cornea's curved shape does a lot but tiny muscles must adjust the shape of the lens to complete the job. Eyeballs are not all the same shape, though. Sometimes, the eyeball is too long or too short for the cornea and lens to bend the light rays just the right amount to make them focus on the retina. If you wear glasses or contacts, you know that one solution is to use a lens to assist the eye. Now, the excimer laser is making it possible for people who don't want to—or whose careers don't allow them to—wear glasses or contact lenses to have their vision permanently improved by surgery.

Through this innovative procedure called photo-refractive keratectomy (PRK), the excimer laser reshapes the cornea. It's possible to do such delicate sculpturing of the human eye because the excimer laser can remove microscopically thin sections of the cornea. And since the excimer laser emits short, high-energy pulses of cool ultraviolet radiation, there isn't any heat damage to surrounding tissue.

The PRK procedure is in the final testing stages in the United States. There has been concern that this process could permanently scar the eye, causing clouded vision. There is also the chance of swelling, tissue damage, and a natural return of vision problems. So far, though, tests in Europe as well as in the United States have been successful for most patients. For some, vision has even improved to the point where they no longer need glasses or contacts at all.

Here the doctor is reshaping the patient's cornea.

(COURTESY OF DR. KEITH THOMPSON)

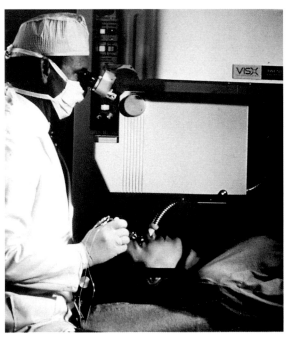

TACKLE THE CHALLENGE

YOUR CHALLENGE: *In what ways other than surgery might an excimer laser be useful? To get you started, think of ways that being able to make precise cuts without generating heat could be used in manufacturing cars and in creating the circuits on tiny computer chips.*

Lasers have many uses, including reading bar codes on items at supermarket checkout stands, creating invisible fences, and reading compact discs (CDs) to play music. Sometimes, though, lasers are just for fun.

This image projected on Stone Mountain near Atlanta, Georgia, is part of a laser show. To create this image, an artist first drew a line drawing. Next, different points on that drawing were touched, to enter their position into the memory of a computer. The computer drives mirrors that aim a laser beam at those points. Like connecting a dot-to-dot puzzle, this traces the outline of the drawing. The pattern is retraced over and over so quickly that it gives the illusion of being a solid, glowing outline. By tracing one pattern and then another slightly different pattern and then yet another pattern, the laser-generated images give the illusion of moving. To create more complex images during the laser show, three different laser beams are used to scan slightly different patterns of points at the same time.

SEE FOR YOURSELF

Try this to see for yourself how a laser light beam creates the illusion of generating a solid glowing outline by connecting points. You'll need a flashlight and a really dark room. Switch on the flashlight, and aim it straight ahead into the darkness. Imagine a big triangle suspended in the air in front of you and touch the three points of that triangle, one after the other, with the flashlight's bright beam. Next, quickly move through a pattern, connecting each of those points over and over. As long as you cycle the light through the pattern quickly enough, you'll see a solid triangle-shaped outline apparently suspended in the air.

Now ask a friend to work with you. Have your friend use a second flashlight to create a different image, such as a circle, so it appears in the same space as your triangle. How do the combined images look? What do you suppose would happen to the light beams and the images they create if you covered the end of the flashlight with red or blue cellophane? Try it.

Just for fun, you could combine light and music and your creativity to put on a light show for your family and friends.

(COURTESY OF BATTELLE'S PACIFIC NORTHWEST LABORAT

Manny may look and act like a person in many ways, but he's a robot—one with very special features. Take a close look at Manny's skin, for example. This flexible rubber has a temperature-control system that keeps Manny's body at 98.6 degrees Fahrenheit—normal human body temperature. And sensors attached to this skin let Manny detect environmental changes. Then he reports these changes in an electronic voice.

PROBLEM Some jobs, such as testing how well protective clothing will shield workers against harmful chemicals, are too dangerous for people to perform.

SCIENCE RESCUE Get a robot to do the job.

It took more than three years and over $2.5 million for scientists at Battelle's Pacific Northwest Laboratory to build a robot to stand in for human volunteers for the United States Army. But Manny, as this 5-foot-11, 165-pound robot is called, is very special indeed. Unlike most robots, which may be no more than arms with tools in place of hands, Manny has a human shape. Using more than forty computer-controlled joints and a support arm attached to his back, Manny is able to simulate walking, creeping, and crawling motions while testing fire-protective clothing and gear designed to protect people against harmful chemicals, such as might be used in chemical warfare.

Manny also "sweats" a liquid containing all the same chemicals as human perspiration from tiny tubes which are two to three inches apart on the rubber skin covering his body. Manny tests new gas mask designs too. He can simulate inhaling and exhaling by having his chest expand and contract faster or slower depending on whether he is supposed to be running or walking. No air is "inhaled" by the robot, but a hose connected to a pressurized air line lets Manny "exhale." This exhaled air is even injected with water vapor to make it have the same typical moisture content as human breath.

Despite his ability to simulate human activities, Manny is only a machine. A robot's ability to move is provided by electric power, pneumatic power (parts made to operate by compressed air), or hydraulic power (parts made to operate by compressed liquid). A robot's actions are controlled by a computer that has been programmed by a human being.

(COURTESY OF FORD MOTOR CO

Do you see the big metal arms on either side of the car being built? These are industrial robot welders. They're capable of doing the same job over and over with the same precise results—without getting tired or needing a dinner break. They can even work overtime if necessary.

The MicroVER looks like a miniature torpedo. Just under five inches in diameter and only twenty-five inches long, it's the perfect size to slip inside pipelines to search for cracks or valve problems and to inspect possible hazards in places such as nuclear reactor facilities. A tether cable supplies the MicroVER with power and connects it to a work station. There, safe and comfortable, the robot's human partner watches a color monitor to see through the robot's camera eye, and guides its moves by manipulating a joystick.

Such robot and human teams may one day make it possible for people to stay safe while performing tasks in dangerous environments. For example, the human worker could be comfortably on board a ship while the robot partner is on the ocean bottom working on an oil well–drilling operation. Or doctors might be able to use robot "hands" to provide surgical treatment even to remote regions of the world. Special gloves already exist that let a human worker's motions send signals to a computer that translates them into robot maneuvers. The doctor could view the patient through a robot's camera eye while going through motions for a surgical procedure that the robot would actually perform.

(COURTESY OF BENTHOS, INC.)

21

YOUR CHALLENGE: *Plan what steps a tabletop robot arm would need to go through to pick up five one-inch cubes and arrange them in a semicircle on a fourteen-by-ten-inch piece of paper. Every year the Society of Manufacturing Engineers holds a robotics contest with divisions for middle school students, high school students, and college students. This was one of the challenges for this contest.*

Even if you don't have access to the materials to actually build a robot arm, write a step-by-step list of what moves it would have to go through to perform the contest challenge. As you develop your list, think about these points:

1. What moves will the arm need to go through to pick up a block?
2. What motions would the arm need to make to position a block?
3. What would the robot arm need to do to release the block?

In the real contest, the finished robot arm—like a real robot—is connected to a computer that is programmed to make it perform the job. Remember that directing a robot is like giving orders to an alien. You can't simply tell an alien to make a peanut-butter-and-jelly sandwich, for example, because it wouldn't have any idea how to do it. You'd have to tell the alien to go to the pantry, get out a jar of peanut butter, set the jar on the counter, unscrew the lid, take off the lid, set the lid on the counter, get a loaf of bread, open the bread wrapper, and so forth.

If you'd like to actually build a robot or a robot arm, write or call the following manufacturers for information on robotics kits designed especially for beginners: Kelvin Electronics, Ken Hub Drive, Melville, New York 11747, telephone 1-800-645-9212, or Pitsco, P.O. Box 1328, Pittsburgh, Kansas 66762, telephone 1-800-835-0686 (in Kansas 1-800-842-0581).

If you're in middle school or higher and would be interested in knowing more about the annual robotics contest, write to Robotics Contest, Society of Manufacturing Engineers, One SME Drive, Box 930, Dearborn, Michigan 48121. The Society of Manufacturing Engineers allows middle school and high school contestants to use kits to construct their robotics entries.

YOUR CHALLENGE: *Plan and draw a diagram of a robot that could move around on Mars. Not sure what the surface of Mars is like? Take a close look at the picture that was taken by the Viking 2 probe* **(right).**

This strange-looking vehicle is a test model for the Russian Mars Rover. The finished Mars Rover is scheduled to land on Mars in 1997. There, a long way from human help, an on-board computer will respond to obstacles and direct the Mars Rover's exploration of the Red Planet. To help it navigate the alien rocky terrain, the body of the Mars Rover is in three segments capable of moving independently. And the cone-shaped wheels are designed for the best possible traction.

(COURTESY OF C. ANDERSON, THE PLANETARY SOCIETY)

Mars' ground is believed to be similar to a rocky desert on Earth. The atmosphere on Mars is much thinner than Earth's and composed mainly of carbon dioxide, the waste gas people and animals breathe out. Dust storms may go on for weeks, with winds blowing up to 170 miles per hour.   (COURTESY OF NASA)

(COURTESY OF SABOLICH PROSTHETIC & RESEARCH)

It may surprise you when you notice that one of Sarah East's legs isn't real. Normally this leg is covered by a soft plastic shell that makes it look almost real. Sarah certainly acts as though both her legs are her own. Besides running, she jumps, rides a bicycle, dances, and even plays softball on a little league team.

PROBLEM   A child who has had a leg amputated wants to be able to run and play.

SCIENCE RESCUE   Create an artificial leg with a knee joint that works like the real thing and electronic sensors in the foot that trick the brain into "feeling" the foot hit the ground.

Sarah East is able to use her artificial leg so naturally because it's made of a lightweight plastic and has a special knee joint called the Oklahoma City running knee. This innovative artificial knee joint, developed by John Sabolich of the Sabolich Prosthetic & Research Center, is made of lightweight flexible materials developed for the aerospace industry. Cables within this joint make the leg snap back into place after each step, closely simulating the way a normal knee functions. This makes it much easier for the person with the artificial leg to keep a normal leg-to-leg stepping motion—or even a running gait.

If you've ever tried to walk on a leg that was "asleep," you'll be able to appreciate the latest modifications to this special leg—a sense-of-feel system. Pressure sensors in the ball of the artificial foot and in the heel are connected to electrodes in the socket area. When the part of the leg that is left is inserted into this socket, it makes contact with these electrodes. As the person walks, pressure on the sensors causes the electrodes to stimulate the skin.

"It tingles," Sarah explained. "When the front of my leg tingles, I know my toes are touching something, and when the back of my leg tingles, I know my heel is touching." The brain interprets these signals as pressure messages from the foot. Sarah can move even more normally now that she can actually feel when her foot touches the ground. She can even tell how hard she's stepping—the more pressure on the foot, the stronger the sensation.

"It's great," Sarah adds. "I can finally feel my foot."

Here's a closeup look at the special sensors.

(COURTESY MIKE CORRADO, PETROFSKY CENTER FOR REHABILITATION AND RESEARCH)

Some people have their arms and legs but are unable to make them function because of spinal injuries, head injuries, and even certain diseases, such as cerebral palsy. The nerves that relay signals from the brain to the muscles that move the arms or legs aren't successfully delivering those signals. If the spinal cord has been damaged, the nerves may not be receiving those messages at all. Then not only is the person paralyzed, but the muscles become weak from disuse, and other physical problems often develop.

In the photo on the left you can see the system developed by Dr. Jerrold Petrofsky, which allows someone to regain muscle strength and even to walk despite paralyzing spinal injury. What looks like a Walkman attached to the woman's belt is really a computer, sending signals to electrodes embedded in flesh-colored bandages around her leg muscles. In response to impulses from those electrodes, rather than to messages from her brain, her muscles contract and relax much as they normally would. The metal supports on either side of her legs help her muscles support her weight as she stands, and the walker helps her maintain her balance.

Dr. Petrofsky hopes through further research to develop systems that are even less noticeable. More importantly, he wants to develop systems that will help people suffering from nerve damage to be able to function normally again.

TACKLE THE CHALLENGE

YOUR CHALLENGE: *Plan ways your home could be made more "friendly" for someone who has lost the use of his arms or legs or both.*

For one evening, write down the things you do to help prepare dinner, to have fun, and to get ready for bed. Then analyze your list, thinking about what you did that would be more difficult without the use of your arms, your legs, or both your arms and legs. Now plan ways in which your house might be modified to make doing these things easier for someone with that disability.

This demonstration shows how electrodes rather than signals from the brain can cause muscles to contract and relax. In this case the result is finger movement.

(COURTESY OF PETROFSKY CENTER)

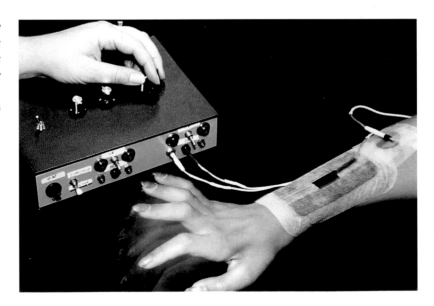

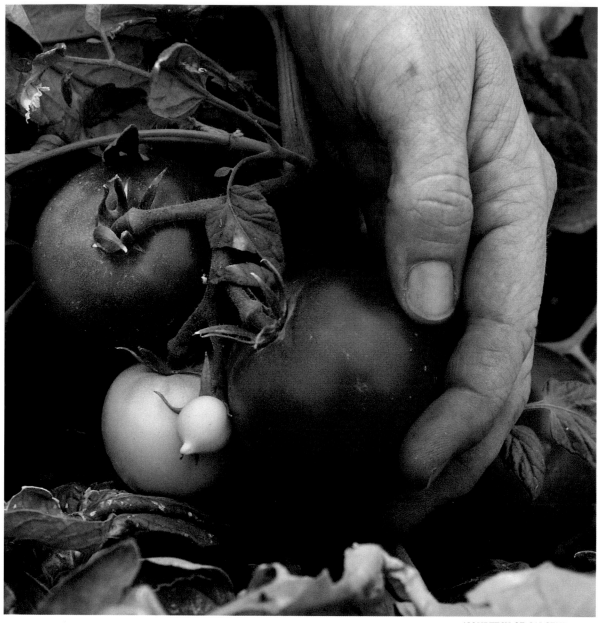

This probably looks like your average tasty tomato, but it isn't. It's a new variety of tomato that ripens more slowly—as much as two weeks more slowly—than normal. That extra time makes it easier for tomato growers and shippers to get the tomatoes to market before they start to rot.

PROBLEM With an ever increasing number of people in the world to feed, we need crops resistant to diseases and insect pests, and easy to ship to market.

SCIENCE RESCUE Genetically engineer plants.

Each cell of every living thing, plant and animal, contains special chemical codes called genes. Every gene is made up of the same four chemicals—adenine, guanine, cytosine, and thymine. But the arrangement of these chemicals and the way they're combined into groups called chromosomes determine what traits or features an organism will have and even what kind of organism it will be. An oak tree produces acorns and is different from a pecan tree, for example, because of its specific genetic code. This genetic code is also important because it determines what characteristics will be passed on to offspring. Each parent gives half of the total number of chromosomes for the offspring they produce.

After many years of research, scientists have been able to identify the location of some of the genes that control specific traits in different organisms, from simple bacteria to plants, animals, and even human beings. And using special chemicals called restriction enzymes, it's possible to extract a segment for a specific gene code. Then, through a complicated process and one of a number of different techniques, researchers are able to introduce the genetic code for a desired trait into a new organism.

In animals, such as fish, the genetic material is inserted into an embryo when it's still made up of only a few cells. In plants, the insertion may be made into a full-grown plant through injection or by misting in the hopes of reaching the seed-producing cells. Or it may be done by inserting the genetic material into tissue cells which can then be grown into a whole new plant. If the process is successful, the animal or plant that develops will have the desired trait controlled by the inserted gene code. And when it reproduces, it will pass this trait on to its offspring.

The new variety of tomato, called FlavrSavr, that you see in the picture was developed by researchers at Calgene in Davis, California, by changing another type of the tomato's genetic code. The hope is that such naturally slow-ripening tomatoes will have a better flavor than those currently available in supermarkets. The usual way to prevent tomatoes from rotting on their way to market is to pick and ship them while they're green. Once they reach the market area, the tomatoes are exposed to ethylene gas, which makes them ripen and change color, but they often still lack flavor.

Actually, the idea of developing new plant

varieties is nothing new. People have been working to improve plants since ancient times. The earliest method was to observe which plants had a desired quality. Then seeds from those plants were saved and planted to produce the next crop. Besides simply observing and saving seeds from the best plants, plant breeders have traditionally also developed hybrid varieties. To do this, the pollen, or male cells, from a plant with one particular quality is transferred to the flower of another plant of the same species. There the male cells unite with the female egg cells to produce seeds that grow into young plants with the characteristics of both parents, including, it is hoped, the desired trait. Unfortunately, it usually takes a very long time, even many years, to breed new plant varieties this way. In the meantime disease-causing organisms may have changed as well, so the newly developed plant variety designed to be resistant to disease is no longer resistant after all.

Because plant breeders want to have more control over plant traits and because they want to develop new plant varieties more quickly, they are now using genetic engineering to change the genetic code in the cells of a plant embryo, to alter the plant that develops from it.

All three of these carp are the same age, but the top one is biggest. While that fish was still in the egg stage, its cells were injected with growth hormone genes from rainbow trout. Such genetically altered carp grow as much as 40 percent faster than normal. Dr. Rex Dunham at Auburn University in Alabama, who developed these transgenic fish, plans to apply what he's learned to develop catfish and other commercial fish that will be ready for market faster.

(COURTESY OF ALABAMA AGRICULTURAL EXPERIMENT STATION, AUBURN UNIVERSITY)

Researchers haven't yet been able to permanently change a human's genetic code. Recently, though, researchers at the National Institutes of Health in Bethesda, Maryland, used gene therapy to help improve a little girl's chances of survival. Her body cells lack the gene that normally causes the body to produce a certain chemical. This chemical destroys poisons that build up naturally as a part of normal body functions. When these poisons go unchecked, the body is not able to produce enough white blood cells, the body's germ fighters, to fight infections. In the past, a child with this gene deficiency had to live in a sterile bubble and usually died before he or she was twenty.

Researchers gave the little girl a gene transplant, injecting her body with cells that contain the missing gene. As hoped, her body responded to this treatment by producing the chemical needed to eliminate the poisons. Since the injected cells eventually die and the little girl's genetic code wasn't permanently changed, she'll need a new cell transplant about once a month for her body to function normally.

Researchers hope to find a similar way to help people with other genetic diseases, such as cystic fibrosis (a lung disease) and hemophilia (a disease in which the blood doesn't clot normally in response to an injury).

TACKLE THE CHALLENGE

YOUR CHALLENGE: *Transfer pollen from one species to the flowers of a related species; plant the seeds that are produced to see how cross-pollination affects what the next generation looks like.*

This project can now be done more quickly because extremely fast growing relatives of the mustard plant were developed by Dr. Paul H. Williams, plant pathologist at the University of Wisconsin-Madison. These plants, which sprout, flower, and produce mature seeds in about a month, come in several varieties. For example, one called Basic has dark green leaves, purple stems, and yellow flowers, while another called Variegated has white-and-green leaves. Packets of seeds or entire genetic kits complete with a slow-release fertilizer growing system are inexpensive and available from Carolina Biological Supply Company, 2700 York Road, Burlington, North Carolina 27215. Write or call 1-800-334-5551 for more information.

(COURTESY OF GM HUGHES ELECTRONICS)

This Geo Storm will never run out of gas. Wonder why? Take a close look at the special plug the woman is holding. It's used to plug the car into the recharger that powers up the Geo Storm's special battery. The car was converted to run on electricity rather than gasoline to let General Motors test the technology being developed for electric vehicles.

PROBLEM   Our planet's atmosphere is becoming more polluted and one of the worst contributors is the exhaust from cars, trucks, and buses. But people need to get from one place to another.

SCIENCE RESCUE   Develop nonpolluting vehicles.

Scientists estimate that one of the biggest sources of air pollution in the United States is gas-powered cars. While many states have laws to try to control auto emissions, California is really getting tough. By 1998, two out of every one hundred new cars sold in that state must be emission free.

Electric cars are emission free, but they aren't a perfect solution—at least not yet. The main drawback is that electric cars depend on batteries that have to be recharged about every hundred miles. While some electric cars, like Nissan's Future Electric Vehicle, boast that they can be recharged in as little as fifteen minutes, most take two hours or longer. Electric vehicles also can't be plugged into the average household outlets. The highest voltage available to homes for such heavy duty appliances as stoves or air conditioners is 220 volts. An electric car needs 440 volts to recharge. This means that before electric vehicles can realistically replace gas-powered automobiles as family cars, they will need to be able to recharge much faster and there will have to be conveniently located recharging stations. Still, it may not be many years before people are driving electric cars and stopping at a station to plug in and "charge up."

Another possibility for meeting future transportation needs without emitting polluting exhaust fumes is a superfast train which operates on a system of magnetic levitation, more commonly called maglev. If

you've ever held two bar magnets with like poles close together, you've felt the force pushing the two magnets apart. In one model of maglev train this same like pole reaction is set up between the bottom of the train and the rail. This pushes the train off the track and holds it suspended on a tiny cushion of air. Without wheels rubbing against tracks there isn't any friction to slow the train down, so a maglev train is able to travel very fast—faster than even the current high-speed trains, the Japanese Shinkansen and the French TGV.

(COURTESY OF THYSSEN HENSCHEL, GERMANY)

In the picture above you can see the maglev train, called the Transrapid 07, that's currently being tested in Germany. The Transrapid 07 can travel as fast as 250 miles per hour. This type of maglev train uses standard electromagnets which are placed in a part of the vehicle that curls under a pair of rails. So instead of pushing the train away from the rails, the magnets actually pull the train toward the rails. The problem with this system is that there can be only an extremely tiny gap between the rail and the train. Maintaining such alignment requires constant attention and effort.

Superconductors are materials that let an electric current flow through them in such a way that the charge isn't weakened. When the electric current is flowing, the superconductor also gives off a magnetic field. This field acts like a magnetic mirror. It reflects whatever pole of the magnet is opposite it. Because like poles of magnets repel each other, the cube-shaped magnet floats just above the superconductor (below).

The same process is used to levitate a Japanese maglev test train called the ML500. This train uses superconductive magnets to create the repulsive force that suspends the train above the guide rail. The disadvantage of this system is that superconductive magnets are much more expensive to use than electromagnets because so far they still require extremely cold temperatures to function.

(COURTESY OF IBM RESEARCH)

TACKLE THE CHALLENGE

YOUR CHALLENGE: *Design and build a nonpolluting model car.*

First, collect items you can find around the house that you could use to build the car body, wheels, and axles (rods that connect the wheels). You might want to use an empty pint-size carton or paper cup for the car body. Sturdy cardboard disks or plastic can lids could be used for wheels. And you might want to use straws, pipe cleaners, or pencils for the axles. Of course, you're free to use whatever you can find or think might work well. You'll also want to collect tools, such as scissors, and materials, such as tape and paper brads, that could help you assemble your model car.

Once you have a collection of building materials, think about what kind of car you could build with them. Remember, the friction of pushing through the air as well as the friction between the wheels and the roadway will slow your car down. So you may want to think about shaping your car so it will slip through the air with the least resistance. You'll also want to be sure the wheels will be able to turn freely on the axles. This is the time to think about adding power to your car too. What could supply the energy to make the car go without adding any pollution to the air? You might want to think about wind power. Or can you think of a way to have the energy of a wound-up rubber band drive your car?

Next, draw a diagram of your car and think about whether there is anything you might want to change. Finally, build your car, test it, and make any changes you think will improve it.

Here's one model you can build to start your creative juices flowing. Collect the following supplies and then follow the directions. You'll need a clean empty pint carton, two pencils (hexagonal with flat sides), a hole punch, scissors, a rubber band (forming about a three-inch circle unstretched), a six-inch square of quarter-inch-thick Styrofoam, a ballpoint pen, and a compass or a lid that is a two-inch circle.

1. Cut the carton in half lengthwise. Use the half that didn't have the spout opened or use glue to reseal the spout end.
2. On each side of the front (spout) end, make a dot three-fourths of an inch in and one-half inch up. Repeat, making dots three-fourths of an inch in and one-half inch up from the back on both sides. Punch a hole with each dot as the center.
3. Push a pencil into and out of each hole until it slides through freely.
4. Use the compass to draw four two-inch circles on the Styrofoam, or draw around the cap four times. Cut out the circles. Mark a dot in the center of each.
5. Slowly and carefully, poke a pencil point through one circle at the dot. Slide the pencil through the front set of car holes. Slide the pencil through the car so an equal amount sticks out from each side. Then push another circle onto the pencil's point end. Repeat to install the back set of wheels.
6. Snip the rubber band to make one long elastic strip.
7. Cut a notch one-fourth of an inch down from the top of the spout end. Tie one end of the rubber band around the knob above the notch. Tie the other end around the middle of the pencil connecting the back wheels.
8. To power the car, turn the back wheel pencil eight to ten revolutions, winding up

the rubber band. Hold the pencil so the rubber band won't unwind while you place the car on the floor. When you release the pencil, the car will move.

9. Once you've tested this model car, think what you could do to improve it—make it go farther and faster, make it able to carry a load. Test your ideas.

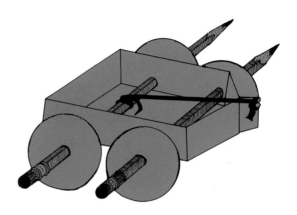

Real vehicles are being developed using a pollution-free power source, a flywheel, that works much like the model windup car. The biggest problem, as you might guess, is that a vehicle powered by a flywheel won't go very far before it has to be recharged. One model being developed in England will only run a few miles at a time, but since it can be recharged in only ninety seconds, there are plans to use it to transport people around shopping areas. Another model being tested by the Lawrence Livermore National Laboratory in California combines a flywheel with a battery for longer runs. There is interest in this car because by 2003 ten percent of all new cars sold in California will, by law, have to be emission free.

Special glass fibers like this one, as thin as a human hair, have greatly improved communication systems.

PROBLEM   There is an ever-increasing number of people who need to be able to communicate with one another.

SCIENCE RESCUE   Develop optical fiber cable to use light to transmit messages.

It may surprise you to learn that Alexander Graham Bell, the inventor of the telephone, was actually the first one to use light, reflected from a sending device to a receiving device, to transmit voice messages. The photophone, as Bell called it, was developed in 1880, four years after the original telephone. Bell's photophone never caught on, though, because it used sunlight, and the reflected light couldn't be bounced very far and still be strong enough to activate the receiver. It also was not possible to use it on a cloudy day.

Although it was known for years that glass would transmit light, glass fibers—strands of glass that were thin, flexible and strong—had to be developed before engineers could take advantage of this. And the fibers had to be very pure glass, because impurities make the light beam scatter, and break up the signal. The first practical optical fiber telephone system began in 1977, connecting Long Beach and Artesia, California.

How does optical fiber transmit a telephone call? When you talk into the phone, your voice pattern is sampled millions of times a second and parts of those samples are then changed into on and off pulses of light. Those pulses are sent along the optical fiber. When the signal has to be sent over a long distance, it's refreshed along the way. At the other end, the pulses are decoded, or changed back into electrical impulses. The machinery in the phone uses these impulses to create the sound waves that an ear interprets as your voice. Light pulses can also be used to transmit television pictures and computer information over optical fibers.

These are the drawings submitted by Alexander Graham Bell when he patented his photophone. A reflector was used to direct sunlight through a lens to a mechanism that vibrated as someone spoke into the phone. Next, the pulses of light which were emitted into the air were caught at the receiving end by a large disk. When the light touched a special detector in the disk, the light energy was transformed into electrical current which, like Bell's original phone, caused vibrations that set up waves of air—sounds.
(COURTESY AT&T ARCHIVES)

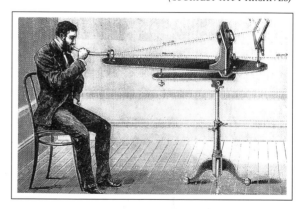

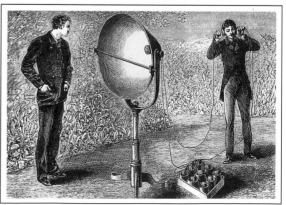

The thin optical wires shown in this picture can transmit signals for twenty-four thousand telephone calls all at once. That's the same amount as all these bundles of copper wires. So optical fiber takes up much less space. It's also much lighter—only a quarter pound for a mile of fiber compared to thirty-three tons of copper wire needed for the same information-carrying capacity.

An optical fiber is made up of two slightly different types of glass—the core glass and the surrounding glass, called the cladding. Light naturally reflects or refracts (bends) when it moves from one type of glass to another. With the right two types of glass, the cladding glass reflects the light, keeping it inside the core as it travels through the fiber. The cladding is coated with a tough plastic covering to help shield it from dust and scratches.

(COURTESY OF CORNING, INC.)

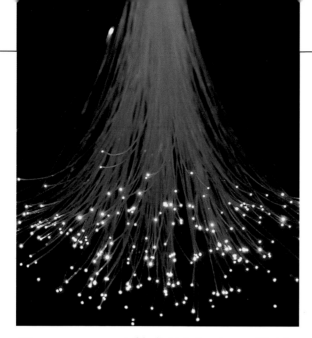

Here you can see visible light being transmitted by optical fibers. (COURTESY CORNING, INC.)

SEE FOR YOURSELF

This activity will let you discover for yourself what this photo illustrates—that light really is transmitted through optical fiber. You'll need a pen flashlight, two yards of monofilament fishing line, scissors, a sheet of black construction paper, and transparent tape. Cut the fishing line into lengths about six inches long. Arrange these in a bundle and wrap one end with tape to hold it together. Next, switch on the pen light in a dark room. Lay the paper on a tabletop or on the floor. Hold the flashlight about a foot away and aim the light at the paper. Hold one end of the bundle of monofilament strands against the light. The strands will glow, emitting tiny beams of light that will show up as dots on the paper. If you were to look at an actual optical fiber cable, you wouldn't be able to see the light pulses, though. These signals are in the infrared light range. This light is the least likely to scatter and weaken but infrared is invisible to the human eye.

TACKLE THE CHALLENGE

YOUR CHALLENGE: *Collect the materials listed below. Then see what you can create to communicate with a partner who is on the opposite side of a one- or two-story house.*

Collect the following items: a full roll of monofilament fishing line, 3 paper cups, 4 buttons, 3 pocket mirrors, 4 sheets of plain white paper, a softball, 6 rubber bands, 3 flashlights, and a pencil. It isn't necessary to use all of these items, but this is all you can use. You may have two friends help in addition to the person with whom you communicate. Brainstorm a list of possible ways to communicate. Pick the idea you think is the most likely to be successful. Then check your idea with an adult to be sure it's likely to be safe for you and not destructive to the property before you develop your design and experiment to test your idea.

Here are a couple of ideas to start you thinking. You could wrap a paper message around a softball, securing it with a rubber band, and toss the ball over the house. Or, with careful planning and trial-and-error testing, you could position a friend at a point halfway around the side of the house and flash a coded light signal that the friend passes on. In fact, in the 1870s the army used a heliograph, a device that has a reflective surface, to transmit a coded message with flashes of light. A whole network of these let a message be relayed nearly fifty miles. The navy currently blinks light messages with a signal lantern.

When Hurricane Hugo roared ashore along the southeastern coast of the United States in September 1989, the wind blew steadily at speeds up to 135 miles per hour. In August 1992 Hurricane Andrew had sustained wind speeds as great as 145 miles per hour when the storm was at its maximum intensity just east of the Bahama Islands. It's no wonder such powerful storms smash houses like this one, tear out big trees, and toss ships onto the shore.

PROBLEM   Hurricanes and tornadoes, the fiercest storms on earth, cause tremendous property damage and kill many people every year.

SCIENCE RESCUE   Build an improved system of satellites and radar stations to detect these storms in time to warn people who are likely to be in their path.

In this satellite view of Hurricane Hugo, the cloud pattern reveals the cycling winds typical of such giant storms. A computer program accurately predicted that Hurricane Hugo would travel inland two hundred miles to West Virginia; this prediction provided people in Hugo's path time to protect their property and move to shelters out of the strike zone. In the same way, people in Florida and Louisiana were warned in time to prepare for Hurricane Andrew.

(COURTESY OF NOAA)

The largest storms in the world, hurricanes often stretch across hundreds of miles, travel thousands of miles, and last for more than a week before they run out of destructive energy. Hurricane winds may average more than 100 miles per hour. Some, like Hurricane Andrew, have winds that blow steadily at over 150 miles per hour with gusts at nearly 175 miles per hour. Heavy rains and wind-driven waves cause flooding and add to the storm's damage.

Heat and moisture are the key ingredients in producing a hurricane. The sun's heat warms the ocean, causing water to evaporate or change from a liquid to a gas called water vapor. This mixture of water vapor and warmed air naturally rises. The higher it goes, the more the air is cooled until the water vapor condenses or turns back into a liquid, releasing heat into the air in the process. For this reason, the atmosphere heats up wherever there is a thunderstorm.

A hurricane forms when a cluster of storms develop close together. As these storms generate heat, air within the storm becomes warmer and rises, causing air pressure, or the amount of air close to the surface, to lower. Immediately, air rushes in from all sides to replace the rising air. The more heat generated by the storm, the more quickly air moves, creating powerful winds. Because the storm mass that becomes a hurricane covers a fairly large area and continues for some time, the earth's rotation affects the wind direction. In the Northern Hemisphere, those winds spiral counterclockwise. If the wind speed reaches seventy-four miles per hour or stronger, the storm is officially classified as a hurricane.

(COURTESY OF NOAA)

Tornadoes, like the one in this picture, are also destructive storms. A tornado is produced when a hot, moist air mass becomes trapped by a cold, dry air mass. Usually the cold air mass pushes in under a rising warm mass. Sometimes, though, the cool air may settle on top of the warm air. As the warm air struggles upward, a tongue of the hotter air may break through, creating a tunnel in the cooler air mass above it. Suddenly, the warm air rushes up into the tunnel. More air sweeps in from all sides to replace this rapidly rising air. The rising air naturally rotates within the parent storm. And the tornado that's produced by this storm will whirl in the same direction as the parent storm. Usually that's counterclockwise, but on rare occasions a tornado may spin clockwise.

Tornadoes are likely to have even stronger winds than hurricanes—sometimes as fast as 350 miles per hour. Luckily, this destructive force attacks a much smaller area—rarely more than a few hundred yards across. The storm also only lingers for about thirty seconds, instead of hours, before whirling on. Of course, with such powerful winds, that's long enough.

The key to helping people protect themselves from storms is to warn them a storm is coming. Satellites provide images of clouds over the earth plus information about the atmosphere's temperature and water-vapor content. This helps meterorologists, people who study the weather, to spot hurricanes and conditions likely to produce severe storms. Then, using wind speed and direction of cloud movement, and with the help of computers, the experts are able to model the storm's path and predict, in time to issue warnings, where the storm is likely to strike.

This is one of the United States' new-generation GOESs (Geostationary Operational Environmental Satellites). While earlier weather satellites could either take pictures or monitor the atmosphere's temperature and water-vapor fields, a GOES can do both at the same time. (COURTESY OF NOAA)

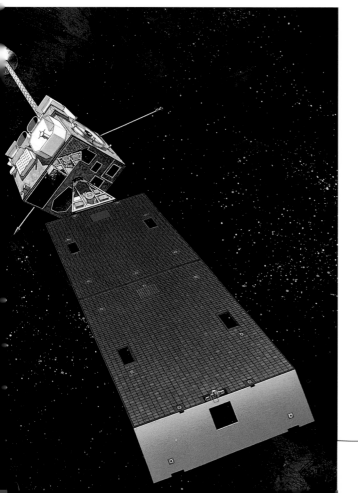

In the past, people weren't warned of an approaching tornado until a funnel cloud was spotted. Now NEXRAD, which stands for next generation weather radar, is being used to create a whole network on alert for early signs of these superstorms. NEXRAD sends out radio waves that are bounced back when they strike raindrops. These echoes are then picked up by an antenna. By studying how much the frequency of the radio waves (the number of radio waves per minute) changes, a meterorologist can determine if the air containing the raindrops is moving toward or away from the NEXRAD site and how quickly it's moving. When the signals show raindrops both moving toward and away from the radar at the same time, the twisting funnel of a tornado could be forming and a warning is quickly issued to the area in danger.

TACKLE THE CHALLENGE

YOUR CHALLENGE: *Design a severe storm preparedness kit for your family.*

Plan what your family would need to have on hand if the power went off, if your community's water supply was cut off, and if it wasn't possible to purchase food for several days. Don't forget a small battery-powered radio to keep up with the latest weather news. Also consider that someone could be injured during the storm, so think about what first aid supplies might need to be included. Next, assemble this kit. Talk with your family about the best place to keep your severe storm preparedness kit.

(COURTESY OF IBM RESEARCH)

In the top picture you can see how a computer chip looks when you view it through an optical microscope. The most powerful optical microscopes are capable of magnifying about two thousand times. In the second photo you can see how this same computer chip looks through an electron microscope. With an electron microscope it's possible to magnify objects up to three hundred thousand times. Finally, in the third photo, you can see this same computer chip as viewed with a scanning tunneling microscope (STM). This special tool makes it possible to actually explore the surfaces of the atoms that make up the chip.

SCIENCE RESCUE Invent the scanning tunneling microscope (STM) to provide an atom-by-atom view of the surface of materials where interactions take place.

PROBLEM When one material comes in contact with another, sometimes a reaction happens that causes problems. For example, acid rain, rain that is more acidic than normal, reacts with rocks to release larger than usual amounts of metals, such as aluminum and lead, into the soil and water. The effect can be toxic to plants and animals.

Sometimes the rescue comes first, meaning that scientists develop a new tool and then discover how it can be used to solve problems. That was the case with the scanning tunneling microscope. For the first time, this special kind of microscope made it possible to see a profile of the atoms making up the surface of materials. Scientists interested in learning what happens when materials interact found the STM would let them study the surfaces where those interactions take place. And researchers trying to understand the structure of a material discovered they could use the STM to actually see how the atoms on the surface of that material are arranged.

To scan surfaces at the atomic level, the STM has a needle probe sharpened to a point that's just one atom wide. This probe works inside a chamber from which all the air has been removed so that no air molecules will bump into it. As this special needle moves across the surface of a material, an electric current flows from its tip. If the material is able to conduct electricity or is coated with something that can, electrons (tiny charged particles) flowing from the needle will bump into the electrons of the material's atoms. A computer detects when the needle's electrons strike the surface. The computer then uses this information to project a visual image that corresponds to an atom-by-atom profile of the surface of the material. A variation of this microscope, the atomic force microscope (AFM), makes it possible to see the surface of materials that don't conduct electricity.

Scientists have also found that by bringing the tip of the STM's probe even closer to a surface, atoms can be moved one at a time. In the future, this technique might be used to create entirely new materials. Or it might be used to arrange circuits on computer chips so they're much smaller than anything produced today. It might even be used to "see" what happens to cells when disease organisms attack so new cures can be developed.

The probe scans the surface atom by atom.

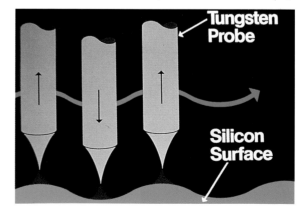

Tungsten Probe

Silicon Surface

YOUR CHALLENGE: *Pretend you are having a party. You want to include apple slices as part of a fruit tray, but sliced apples quickly turn brown. How can you keep the apple slices looking fresh?*

First, you need to understand that the flesh of an apple turns brown as a result of its molecules reacting with the oxygen in the air. To prove to yourself that this color change is strictly on the surface, use a plastic knife to slice off a piece of apple and let it set until it turns brown. Then use the knife to scrape off a thin layer of the apple's surface; you'll discover that just underneath the fruit is still light-colored. So the trick to keeping apple slices looking fresh is to keep the surface from coming in contact with the air. Your challenge is to figure out what you can use to protect the surface of the apple slices that will be safe to eat and won't spoil the taste.

Now, brainstorm. Think of things you might use to coat the apple slices. Look in your refrigerator and pantry to help you think of possibilities. Be sure to check with an adult to be sure anything you decide to try is safe to eat. Some things you might try are orange juice, vegetable oil, and salt water.

Next, set up your test. Work on a clean cutting board. Be sure the slices are all from the same type of apple and that each is about the same thickness. Have your test coatings ready and work quickly to cover the slices. Put one coating on each slice and set it on a paper towel labeled with the name of the coating. Set one slice aside uncoated. This will be your control. Check your slices every five minutes for twenty minutes, writing down when each slice turns brown, if it does. Finally, taste any slice that is still fresh-looking, and decide which has the best flavor.

Analyze your results. If all of your apple slices turned brown, what else could you try as a protective coating? If you didn't like the taste, what similar substance might protect the apple without detracting from the flavor? How might the scanning tunneling microscope help you find a better way to slow the apple's interaction with oxygen in the air?

SCIENCE AND TECHNOLOGY: PARTNERS IN INVENTION

No matter what a person may dream up, an invention can only be built using the technology that is currently available. For example, Leonardo da Vinci was a noted inventor who lived in the fifteenth century. That was long before electricity had been investigated and harnessed. So when he devised the idea of an automatic spit to turn roasting meat, he couldn't simply hook the spit up to an electric motor. Instead he used hot air rising from the cooking fire to turn a fan in the chimney. This cycling fan in turn made the spit rotate.

Even your most far-fetched ideas may one day develop into working inventions when technology catches up to you. So don't let a single idea slip away. Keep an idea journal. Be sure to include drawings of what you think your invention should look like.

Keep watching for new product reports on television, in newspapers, and in magazines. There are new discoveries being made all the time.

But don't worry. Even with all the many solutions you'll learn about, there will still be plenty of problems remaining for you to tackle. And as new tools are developed, they will create new opportunities to improve earlier solutions.

This is an exciting time to be facing the future. Think creatively and keep practicing your problem-solving skills. Who knows, you may one day be the one who recognizes a problem and then brings your knowledge of science to the rescue.

This automatic spit for cooking meat was only one of the many ideas Leonardo da Vinci dreamed up. Some he could never build because technology wasn't yet available to make construction possible.

(COURTESY IBM)

INDEX